Charles Desmarais Gardette

The Whole Truth in the Question of the Fire Fiend

Charles Desmarais Gardette

The Whole Truth in the Question of the Fire Fiend

ISBN/EAN: 9783337309145

Printed in Europe, USA, Canada, Australia, Japan

Cover: Foto ©Andreas Hilbeck / pixelio.de

More available books at **www.hansebooks.com**

THE WHOLE TRUTH

IN THE QUESTION

OF

"THE FIRE FIEND,"

BETWEEN

Dr. R. SHELTON MACKENZIE,

(LITERARY EDITOR OF THE PHILADELPHIA "PRESS,")

AND

C. D. GARDETTE,

BRIEFLY STATED

BY

THE LATTER.

PHILADELPHIA:

SHERMAN & CO., PRINTERS.

1864.

PREFATORY.

Dr. R. Shelton Mackenzie's peculiar code of (literary) morals having caused him to refuse me the opportunity of justification, and withheld him equally from acknowledging his own self-conscious mistakes and misrepresentations in the "*Press*" with reference to the matter between us, I take this method of making known to my friends, and "all whom it may concern," or interest, "the *truth*, the *whole truth, and nothing but the truth*" of the affair, as it relates to the relative positions of Dr. Mackenzie and myself, on the subject of the Poem entitled "The Fire Fiend."

I shall do this as briefly, clearly, and simply as possible; "nothing extenuating, nor setting aught down in malice" (which, I fear, has not been the way the learned literary Doctor will be thought to have treated me), if I know myself, or the merits of my case.

C. D. Gardette.

CORRESPONDENCE, ETC.

On the 30th day of September, 1864, there appeared in the columns of the Philadelphia *Press*, an editorial article, having for its title, "Poe's Raven: Whence came it?"

This article, which was, chiefly, a very unnecessary attempt (and not a particularly brilliant one) to defend the late Edgar A. Poe from the charge of plagiarism, perorated with the following paragraphs, to wit:

"In connection with this affair we may notice a great wrong done to Poe—unconsciously, we hope—by a young gentleman of this city, who has dabbled in literature for some years, but has chiefly made his name known by sending to various newspapers some stanzas entitled 'The Fire Fiend—A Nightmare; from an unpublished manuscript of the late Edgar A. Poe, in the possession of Charles A. Gardette.' These stanzas, which have appeared with the above heading in various newspapers during the last seven years, are somewhat in the manner of 'The Raven,' but are much inferior, in all respects, to that renowned poem, and unworthy of Poe's reputation. We believe that Poe wrote them ;(*) that rejecting them as not good enough for publication, he laid them aside among his failures ; that he subsequently recurred, partly, to their peculiar metre, when composing his 'Raven ;' that the manuscript, found among his papers after his death, was given away to somebody by Mrs. Maria Clemm, his excellent aunt and mother-in-law ; and that this recipient may have been Charles A. Gardette, as aforesaid. A poem which Poe himself had deliberately rejected, and certainly judiciously rejected, should not be cast before the world, from post to pillar, as the fruit of Poe's genius ; but chiefly, it seems, to proclaim, in connection with the name of Poe, the name of the person who holds the manuscript. Thus flies are embalmed in amber crystallization.''

Circumstances prevented my hearing of the above gratuitous attack upon my literary and personal character until the 13th of November, when I immediately wrote to Dr. Mackenzie for a copy of the *Press* containing it, and received the article, cut from that paper, on the 14th, through another *attaché* of the establishment.

Having read Dr. Mackenzie's remarks, I wrote and sent him, on the 15th, a reply, which I requested him to do me the justice of publishing in the *Press* as early as possible.

On the 18th I received from him the following autograph letter :

"1712 Locust Street, November 17th, 1864.

"Sir: When the *Press* was yet young, 'The Fire Fiend, from an unpublished MS. of the late Edgar A. Poe, in the possession of Charles D. Gardette,' was offered me for publication, and by me declined, because, judging from internal evidence, I thought that Poe could not have written it.(ʰ) Neither he, nor you, nor any educated man *could* [all the underscoring is the Doctor's] have written

'And my sweetest incense *is* the blood and tears my victims weep;'

in which plural nouns and a verb in the singular so palpably break Priscian's head.(ᶜ)

"I have an impression that the poem appeared in the *Evening Journal* of this city, after I declined it. Then it was published in the New York paper, which I never saw, though I knew the fact, and in the *St. Augustine Examiner*, December 6th, 1860, as I find from a MS. copy thereof [Query: of the poem, or of the *Examiner?* G.], sent me at the time, which is now before me. [Query: does he mean that the time, viz., December 6th, 1860, is *now* before him ? G.] I have always believed that *you* sent it, for surely no one else could care to copy such a long poem. So much for that point. " As to the other,—that Poe did write 'The Fire Fiend,' that Mrs. Clemm gave it away, that Poe rejected it, and that you held it,—*I* am not the person to be assailed.(ᵈ) Some months ago, a correspondent of the *Times* (London) published a letter therein, in which he accused Poe of having translated 'The Raven' from an Oriental poem. . . . . One of the London journals defending Poe, said, that if he stole from any one, it was from himself, for that he had written a poem called the 'Fire Fiend,' which he had rejected, but on which he drew for the metre and the manner of ' The Raven,' and that Poe's mother-in-law had given the MS. to a gentleman in Philadelphia. Naturally enough I thought that *you* were the recipient, and said so. . . . .

" If you desire it, your letter shall appear in the *Press* on Monday, followed by a note of mine, to the effect of what I now have told you. I take leave, in all good feeling, to suggest the omission of the paragraph which states that Poe never rejected the 'Fire Fiend,' 'though he might have rejected it, had it ever chanced to come within the sphere of his critical observation.'(•) This affirms a new and illogical theory, that the writer of a poem is not naturally a critic upon it, with power to reject or publish it.

" I have to add that I am sorry to learn from you that what I hastily wrote, without any unfriendly feeling, has been offensive to you. I would suggest that you give the public a history of the ' Fire Fiend,' and how it came into your possession,(ᶠ) for where such a man as Poe is charged with having written such a feeble poem, the mere assertion of any gentleman that he holds its manuscript, will not and ought not be accepted as proof of authorship.(ᵍ)

" Your obedient servant,
" R. SHELTON MACKENZIE."

To this letter I made an immediate reply, stating in substance, what is reproduced by the Doctor as its contents, in his published "explanation" (given below), and one thing, in addition, which he does *not* reproduce, viz.,

that I affirmed the line, "And my sweetest incense is
the blood and tears my victims weep," to be *grammatically correct*, and was willing to stake my claims as an
"educated man" on its correctness.

On the 21st of November, Dr. Mackenzie published
my first letter to him, and added to it what he called
"a few sentences of explanation." Here is the combined
article, as it appeared in the *Press* of November 21st.

"LITERARY COUNTERFEITING.

"To the Editor of the Press.

"Sir: Owing to long absence from town, it was but a day or
two ago that I became aware of the use (or, more properly, abuse)
of my name in an article under the heading above quoted, in *The
Press* of September 30th.

"Pray permit me to correct a few errors into which the writer
of that article has fallen—'unconsciously, I hope'—with regard
both to the MS. poem (the 'Fire Fiend') to which he therein
alludes, and to myself. The writer of that article asserts that I
have been 'sending to various newspapers some stanzas, entitled
the "Fire Fiend," &c.' I assure the writer that I never sent, caused
to be sent, or knew of the sending of the stanzas alluded to, to any
other newspaper than the New York *Saturday Press*, to which I
gave them at the request of the then editor, Mr. Henry Clapp, Jr.

"And, had the writer seen the said stanzas in that journal—
where they were originally and only published by me—and read
the editorial note by which they were prefaced therein, he would
have been spared the perpetration of his ingenious and ingenuous (?)
criticism.

"The writer further states that the said stanzas 'have appeared
in various newspapers during the last *seven years*.' I assure him
that, if this be true, it is an authentic case of modern miracle, in-
asmuch as I have the best of all possible reasons for believing that
the said stanzas were never in type previous to their publication in
the New York *Saturday Press*, which was in the winter of 1859-60.

"The writer asserts that 'a great wrong' has been done to Mr.

Poe by the 'casting before the world, from post to pillar, a poem which Poe himself had deliberately and judiciously rejected.'

"I assure the writer that Mr. Poe never deliberately, nor in any other manner, 'rejected' the poem of the 'Fire Fiend.' I feel constrained to add, however, that I think it extremely probable he would have rejected it, had it ever chanced to come within the sphere of his critical observation.

"The writer's pleasant irony on the subject of my literary reputation, and the brilliant and original simile with which he adorns it, I pass cheerfully over. It has not hurt me much, and its composition was doubtless a relief to his feelings.

"The motive, too, to which he so shrewdly (!) attributes my 'casting from post to pillar,' &c., the said poem,—viz., a desire to 'proclaim, in connection with the name of Poe, the name of the person holding the manuscript'—I am disposed to treat with equal mildness. But, as he himself has—'unconsciously,' I suppose—assisted to spread still further the said 'connection,' I think he might, at least, have given my name correctly. To the best of my knowledge and belief, my middle initial is D, and not A.

"However, I even forgive him this, also, and will merely state, in conclusion, that the *MS.* of the '*Fire Fiend*' was *never* 'laid aside,' nor 'subsequently recurred to' by Mr. Poe; that it was *not* 'found among his MSS. after his death;' that it was *not* 'given away to somebody by Mrs. Clemm' (who never saw it in MS.); and that the undersigned was *not* such a 'recipient' of the said manuscript as the aforesaid writer believes he may have been.

"Respectfully, &c.,

"C. D. Gardette.

"November 15, 1864."

["The writer of the above, son of a respectable dentist in this city, thinking himself aggrieved by our mention of his name some weeks ago, has appealed to our sense of justice to allow his denial or defence to appear. Granting his request, it is necessary to add a few sentences in explanation.

"Some months ago a letter appeared in the *Times*, charging the late Edgar A. Poe with having plagiarized 'The Raven' from an Oriental poem, and comments on this accusation were made by 'The Lounger' of the *Illustrated Times*, Mr. 'Flaneur' of the

Morning Star, the editor of *The Reader*, and, we believe, in other London papers. One of these writers mentioned the *on dit* that Poe had written a poem, in a metre resembling that of 'The Raven;' that, having laid it aside as not good enough for publication, he had worked some of its lines into 'The Raven,' and that the manuscript of the rejected poem was in possession of a gentleman of Philadelphia, to whom Poe's mother-in-law (Mrs. Clemm) had given it. On this subject we wrote an article, vindicating Poe from the charge of plagiary,[?] and mentioning that the other poem alluded to had repeatedly, within the last seven years, been published under the title of 'The Fire Fiend: A Nightmare—from an unpublished manuscript of the late Edgar A. Poe, in the possession of Charles D. Gardette.' We attributed this frequent publication to a desire, on Mr. Gardette's part, to have his name publicly associated with Poe's, and said that flies were sometimes thus preserved in amber crystallization,—a remark not in the best taste, nor at all original.

"Our strong impression, amounting to a belief, is that 'The Fire Fiend' was offered for publication in *The Press*, and declined, because we did not believe that Poe had written it.(h) He never *could* have said 'The blood and tears my victims weep *is* my sweetest incense,' for he always wrote grammatically.(i) We have also believed that 'The Fire Fiend' appeared in the *Evening Journal* in this city before it was published in the New York *Saturday Press*, in which, however, we did not see it, and therefore missed 'the editorial note' referred to. But it did also appear in the St. Augustine *Examiner*, December 16th, 1860, for a manuscript copy, avowedly made from that paper, is before us, and we reasonably thought that Mr. Gardette, whose middle initial is D, not A, had sent it to us. We are not quite satisfied that our impression is incorrect. We cannot implicitly rely on Mr. Gardette's assertion until he shows how this 'unpublished manuscript of the late Edgar A. Poe' came into 'the possession of Charles D. Gardette;' shows, also, that it *is* one of Poe's manuscripts. Up to this time there is nothing but Mr. Gardette's word that it is."(k)

"Since the above was written, we have received a communication from Mr. Gardette (to whom we had privately suggested, for his own sake, that he might withdraw or modify his letter), in which he confesses that 'The Fire Fiend,' which appeared, under his own *imprimatur*, as 'an unpublished manuscript of the late Edgar A. Poe,' in the possession of Charles D. Gardette, 'did not exist even in MS. a fortnight previous to its appearance in the New York *Saturday Press;*' that the editor of that journal knew, when publishing it, that the authorship (imputed) was a hoax, but added a prefatory note pleasantly expressing his own skepticism; that the poem was written and published in consequence of a discussion, followed by a challenge, between its author and a friend about the originality of Mr. Poe's genius, which, it was contended, rendered a successful literary counterfeit of his productions impossible, and that, therefore, Mr. Poe never laid eyes upon said poem. Mr. Gardette actually congratulates himself on the counterfeit having 'been enough like Poe in manner and matter to have deceived several literary critics on both sides of the Atlantic.' In this he is wrong. One English critic seems to have merely *heard* of the forged poem, and we venture to affirm that no one in this country carefully read it without doubts of its authenticity.([1]) Lastly, Mr. Gardette offers us a succinct and authentic history of the composition and authorship of the 'Fire Fiend,' together with many other details he happens to know in connection with it. We decline this detailed confession of a literary fraud, and advise Mr. Gardette to confine it to his own bosom.([m]) There is nothing wrong in imitating an author's style, but what can justify publishing an imitation, as from the dead author's own manuscript, and doing his memory the great injustice of not confessing the 'hoax' for four or five years? We dismiss this painful subject, with no intention of returning to it.]—Ed. Press.''

The tone and style of Dr. Mackenzie's "sentences of explanation" in the above article, as well as the errors and misrepresentations they contained, appeared to me to demand a prompt reply, and consequently, on the 22d, I addressed him the following letter, to wit:

"910 Walnut Street, Nov. 22d, 1864.
" R. Shelton Mackenzie, Esq.

"Sir: Your intention, as expressed in this morning's *Press*, to dismiss and not recur again to the subject between us, you will, I trust, find cause to modify after reading this communication.

"Your comments, in your journal of to-day, upon my letters, &c., are written in a petty spirit of injustice, which I should have thought beneath a gentleman of your age and experience. For example, Sir : in your *private* note of November 17th, to me, you *correctly* quoted a line from the 'Fire Fiend,' and pronounced it, *as thus quoted,* 'ungrammatical,' and unworthy an 'educated man.' I replied to you, that the line was *grammatically correct,* and offered to stake my claims as an educated man on its accuracy. Now, sir, in your *published* comments of this morning, you *withhold* or *ignore that* portion of my letter, while you deliberately *misquote* the line in question,—so reversing it as to make it ungrammatical, which it is *not* as it stands in the poem, or in *your own previous note.* If, sir, you consider this fair and honorable, *I* do not! Nor, I think, will the public, to whom I propose to submit the question.

"Furthermore, you state that you are not yet satisfied that the MS. copy of the poem from the St. Augustine *Examiner* was *not* sent you by me,—in the face of my positive denial. A moment's reflection might have shown you the absurdity of your belief that a man would recopy his own poem from the columns of a distant and obscure newspaper, for the purpose of offering it to another at home, when he had his own MS. to transcribe from. But, really, your insinuation of my untruth is of no consequence. It is a matter of great indifference to me what *you* may think or believe with reference to *myself*, as I do not fancy your opinions will much affect either my literary or social standing.

"But I cannot refrain from observing to you, sir, that you have taken an unwarrantable liberty, in introducing into your remarks the wholly irrelevant subject of my father's profession, and your very unnecessary testimony as to his respectability. Whether I be the son of a dentist, or of a doctor, or of a shoemaker, for that matter, has certainly nothing whatever to do with the subject under discussion. Toward me, who am much your junior, such a style of remark is simply 'little' and undignified. But toward my father, I beg to say, that it very much resembles an impertinence.

"Again : you say, that I 'congratulate' myself on the poem having successfully deceived several critics, &c., &c. This is not true. There is no word of self-gratulation in my note. I said, that I agreed with you as to the inferiority of the poem to that it was intended to resemble, and simply added, that such resemblance had, nevertheless, sufficed to hoax both English and American critics successfully. That this success has been a fact, in spite of your denial, is conclusively proven by an article in the New York *Leader*, for November 19th, 1864, on the subject, which, however, I had not seen at the time I wrote you. But I did not, nor do I specially congratulate myself on so small a matter.

"Finally, sir, though you have an undoubted right to decline my proffered history of the 'Fire Fiend,' you certainly have none to *advise* me as to its publication or withholding. You are not associated, that I am aware, in the monitorship of my 'bosom,' or conscience, nor is your *ipse dixit* on the matter of the 'wrong' of the literary hoax, and its indefensibility, by any means final and without appeal.

"You will or will not publish this letter, as you see fit, of course. It is, however, my intention to give it to the public—if you do not (perhaps, whether you do or not)—together with what other information on the subject I may possess (including your former note to me), at such time as shall be convenient to myself.

"Your obedient servant,

"C. D. GARDETTE."

The above letter was sent, as before stated, to Dr. Mackenzie on the 2♦ of November! Since which date I have heard nothing, directly or indirectly, from him, nor, as far as I know, has anything appeared in the columns of his journal—the *Press*—on the subject.

Therefore, being, of course, unable to compel Dr. Mackenzie to act justly and honorably toward me in the matter, I thus, after due reflection, present the facts of the affair, clearly and succintly, before my friends and the literary public.

I desire, however, before concluding my statement, to make a few comments, draw a few comparisons, and place more immediately before the reader a few points of contrast between the assertions and opinions of Dr. Mackenzie, as uttered at different dates and under different circumstances, on the subject of the "Fire Fiend" controversy. And I shall also reprint an article or two, from journals other than the *Press*, with reference to the poem.

COMMENTS, &c.

For the sake of method and brevity, I have marked such passages in the foregoing correspondence, &c., as I desire the reader to take special note of, by index-letters; and these passages I now propose to speak of, isolating them, and specifying them by means of the aforesaid index-letters. For instance:

(*) September 30. Dr. Mackenzie says, plainly and positively: "*We believe that Poe wrote them!*" (*i. e.*, the stanzas of the "Fire Fiend.")

(ᵇ) November 17. Dr. Mackenzie says, plainly, but not quite as positively, "The 'Fire Fiend' . . . . was by me declined, because . . . . *I thought that Poe could not have written it!*"

(ʰ) November 21. Dr. Mackenzie repeats, plainly, and again positively: "*We did not believe Poe had written it!*"

Reader, what is your opinion of Dr. Mackenzie's value as a lucid and consistent critic?

Again: (ᶜ) November 17. Dr. Mackenzie says: "*Neither Poe nor any educated man* could *have written*, 'And my sweetest incense *is*,' &c. &c. &c."

(ʲ) November 21. Dr. Mackenzie asserts (and very truly) that, "*Poe never* could *have said*, 'The blood and tears my victims weep *is*,' &c. &c. &c."

Reader, can you tell me why the Doctor mentioned

nothing of a grammatical breaking of Priscian's head in any line of the "Fire Fiend," in his article of September 30? When, how, and why he discovered the said head-breaking in the above line, as quoted by him November 17? And why he *reversed* the said line in his re-quotation and re-condemnation of it on November 21? Let me help you by a suggestion. The Doctor says, September 30, that he *believes Poe wrote the poem.* Of course, then, there could be no outrage committed on Priscian therein, because, as the Doctor twice avers, Poe *always* wrote grammatically. But, on the 17th of November, the Doctor wished to state that he had formerly declined the poem because, from "internal evidence," he thought Poe could *not* have written it. So, he, naturally, looked up this "internal evidence," and fell foul of the supposed violence done to Priscian. (I grant you that the dates, here, of the Doctor's two beliefs, make his case rather unsound, and a little conflicting; but all men, even doctors and critics, are fallible.)

As to his *reversion* of the line in his article of November 21, if you recollect that I had, in my reply to his first accusation, asserted the grammatical correctness of the line as it *really stood* in the poem, and also in *his* quotation of November 17; you may, perhaps, fancy that the Doctor had thereupon consulted his Lindley Murray, and had found his friend Priscian in no need of his rather officious, but, no doubt, kindly intended surgery. And that, consequently, still wishing to have a case of it, he— but I leave the inference to your own perspicacity.

Further: (d) The Doctor says, November 17: he is "*not the person to be assailed,*" because an English writer had previously asserted that I had received a rejected MS. of Poe's from Mrs. Clemm, called the "Fire Fiend,"

&c. &c., and that he (the Doctor) only repeated it. But the English critic did not attack me as having done a "great wrong" to Mr. Poe. And the Doctor did! The English critic did not impugn my motives in publishing the said poem. And the Doctor did! The English critic did not make false statements as to the manner and times of the said publication by me. And the Doctor did! The English critic did not affect to doubt my veracity, nor attempt to crush me by irony, nor pass sentence upon me, nor "advise" me as to the affairs of my "bosom." And all these things the Doctor did, as you may read in his articles of September 30 and November 21, and in his private note of November 17. Is he "*not the person to be assailed*," forsooth?

(*ᵉ*) In his note of November 17, the Doctor objects to *my* statement, that "Poe would have, probably, rejected the 'Fire Fiend' if it had ever come within his critical observation," on the ground that it is "*illogical*," to suppose an *author cannot properly criticise his own production* with reference to its rejection. I acknowledge freely that such a theory is illogical; nay, I even think it is positively absurd. But bless you! I didn't fancy I was making any such assertion. Let me put a case to you, Reader. Suppose I had written you, that the poem of "Don Juan" had never come within the sphere of Byron's observation, what would you take me to mean? Would it not dimly occur to you that, possibly, I intended to insinuate that Lord Byron was not the author of "Don Juan?" I think it would—to you, or to "any other man" of average intelligence, except Dr. Mackenzie. But the learned critic did not see it in that light, for with that remark of mine before him, he still insists, with commendable, but somewhat obtuse pertinacity, both in his note of November 17,(ˢ) and in his published comments of November 21(ᵏ) upon my letter of November 15 (in which that remark occurs), that I shall show otherwise than by mere assertion, the " Fire Fiend" to be a genuine MS. of Poe. And yet, as I thought, I had just neatly and delicately confessed that it was nothing of the sort!

(ˢ) Dr. Mackenzie, in his note of November 17, kindly suggests that I "*give the public*" (meaning through his columns, I take it) "*a history of the 'Fire Fiend.'*"

But in his comments of November 21,(ᵐ) he *declines* what he calls—not quite so kindly—my "*detailed confession of a literary fraud,*" and "*advises*" me—his benevolence getting the better of him again—"*to confine it to my own bosom.*"

Now what could have caused this somewhat sudden change in the Doctor's feelings and judgment with regard to the acceptance of the "history," or "detailed confession," do you think? It couldn't be his discovery of the fictitiousness of the poem, for you know he had no belief in its authenticity, as far back even, as the exceedingly misty and uncertain period at which he "declined" it for the *Press*, as he asserts on the 17th, and still again on the 21st of November. The fact that he *did* believe Poe was its author, on the 30th of September, may have had some influence in the matter, though I can't exactly see how. Perhaps, however, you may imagine the question as to the condition of Priscian's head had something to do with it. Well, perhaps so; it certainly is not pleasant to be defrauded by one's own haste out of a capital operation in critical surgery.

(ˡ) Dr. Mackenzie asserts, in his published note of November 21, that only " one English critic seems to have *merely heard* of the forged" (forged is severe!) "poem;" and he " *ventures*" (O! venturesome Doctor!) "*to affirm that no one in this country carefully read it without doubts of its authenticity!*" Now this *latter* affirmation hardly coincides, I " venture" to hint, with the Doctor's own brief but comprehensive statement of September 30,(*) that *he believes Poe wrote them!* referring to the same poem, then called " some stanzas" by the Doctor. And the rest of his above " venture" in the affirmation way will *not* by any means be fully corroborated by the following articles on the subject, extracted respectively from the Philadelphia *Evening Bulletin* and the New York *Leader*, viz. :

[No. 1. From the *Leader*, November 19, 1864.]

" ONE OF POE'S EXPERIMENTS TOWARDS ' THE RAVEN.'

" Under this heading the *Evening Post* of Tuesday has the following :

"' The assertion lately made by a correspondent of the London *Morning Star*, that Edgar A. Poe plagiarized "The Raven" from the Persian, has brought out several letters from a class of Englishmen who look upon that celebrated production as "the greatest single poem that America has ever produced." A writer in *Notes and Queries* indignantly protests against the translation theory, and only hopes that, if it be true, we have more of the same stamp, and done by as competent men as Edgar A. Poe. But the most important result of the discussion is a note from Mr. Macready, the tragedian, part of which we subjoin.

" ' I think the following fantastic poem (a copy of which I inclose), written by the poet whilst experimenting towards the production of that wonderful and beautiful piece of mechanism, "The Raven," may possibly interest your numerous readers. "The Fire-Fiend" (the title of the poem I inclose), Mr. Poe considered incomplete, and threw it aside in disgust. Some months afterwards, finding it amongst his papers, he sent it in a letter to a friend, labelled facetiously, "To be read by firelight, at midnight, after thirty drops of

laudanum." I was intimately acquainted with the mother-in-law
of Poe, and have frequently conversed with her respecting "The
Raven," and she assured me that he had the idea in his mind for
some years, and used frequently to repeat verses of it to her, and
ask her opinion of them frequently, making alterations and im-
provements according to the mood he chanced to be in at the time.'

" ' There are, certainly, remarkable discrepancies between this
account and that which Poe has himself given to the world in
one of the most famous of his critical essays.

" ' The poem which Mr. Macready transmitted to the *Morning Star*
is very long, and contains much which is terrible, ghastly, and too
horrible for print. Its author probably never designed that it
should see the light. We give below the best stanzas, and the
reader will not be slow to discover the presence of that same weird,
wonderful, musical, sensuous harmony, which has made this singular
and erratic genius the head of a distinct school of literature.'

" Here follow the extracts from the poem alluded to, which, we
beg to inform the *Post*, was first printed in the *New York Saturday
Press*, in its issue of November 19, 1859.

" The contributor to that paper accompanied his communication
with the subjoined note, which the reader will please compare with
Mr. Macready's.

" ' PHILADELPHIA, November 6th, 1859.

" ' To THE EDITOR OF THE SATURDAY PRESS.

" ' DEAR SIR: The following fantastic poem was written by Mr.
Poe, while experimenting towards the production of that wondrous
mechanism, "The Raven;" but considering it incomplete, he threw
it aside. Some time afterwards, finding it among his papers, he
inclosed it in a letter to a particular friend, labelled *facetiously*, "To
be read by firelight, at midnight, after thirty drops of laudanum."
How it finally came into the possession of the undersigned, he is not
at present at liberty to tell. The poem is copied *verbatim, literatim,
et punctuatim*, from the original MS.

" ' Yours, &c.,

" 'C. D. GARDETTE.'

" Of course, the whole affair was a hoax."

[No. 2. From the *Evening Bulletin*, November 21st, 1864.]

" Lately a joke, practised in 1859, upon a part of the reading world in this country, has been put upon the English public with great success. A poem purporting to have been an original sketch for the more elaborate picture of 'The Raven' by Edgar A. Poe, was sent to a London newspaper, by Mr. Macready, the actor, who appears to have been deceived by it himself ; for his note accompanying it, which the London editor published with the poem, bears marks of its having been written in entire good faith. The real history of the thing is, that it was written by a gentleman of Philadelphia, and sent to a New York literary paper, not now in existence, the writer accompanying it with the following note :

" ' PHILADELPHIA, November 6th, 1859.
" ' To THE EDITOR OF THE SATURDAY PRESS.

" ' DEAR SIR : The following fantastic poem was written by Mr. Poe, while experimenting towards the production of that wondrous mechanism, " The Raven ;" but considering it incomplete, he threw it aside. Some time afterwards, finding it among his papers, he inclosed it in a letter to a particular friend, labelled *facetiously*, " To be read by firelight, at midnight, after thirty drops of laudanum." How it finally came into the possession of the undersigned, he is not at present at liberty to tell. The poem is copied *verbatim*, *literatim*, *et punctuatim*, from the original MS.

" ' Yours, &c.,
" ' C. D. GARDETTE.'

" The poem was an extremely clever imitation of Poe, but the limited circulation of the *Saturday Press* prevented it from becoming widely known. It has fallen, however, into the hands of Mr. Macready, and he has been the means of hoaxing with it the whole British public, for it has been widely copied in the metropolitan and provincial papers, and has even been accepted as a verity by a number of journals in this country."

The above article from the *Leader* also contained the poem of the " Fire Fiend" in full. But, anxious as I am (or, at least, as Dr. Mackenzie says I am) to have my "name published in connection with that of Poe, as the holder of one of his manuscripts," I have thought it best to withhold the reproduction of this slender link between that brilliant man of genius and myself, on this occasion, and I hope the Doctor will give me credit for the effort such self-denial has cost me.

Readers, and friends, I have now put the case of Mackenzie *vs.* the "Fire Fiend" and its author, fairly before you, I believe, and I really am not very much afraid of your prospective verdict. But while I ask only simple justice for myself, I shall be glad to know that, toward the worthy and venerable Doctor and Critic, your justice is tempered by the mercy which is due to his age and infirmities.

C. D. GARDETTE.

November 28th, 1864.

APPENDIX.

IT occurs to me that a few words of explanation, with reference to the original composition and publication of the "FIRE FIEND," may be appropriately added here, and I therefore add them briefly, as follows:

On a day of November, 1859, a discussion took place between a literary friend and myself, on the subject of Poe's poetic genius. In the course of this discussion, my friend maintained that Poe's marked originality of style, both in thought and expression, rendered difficult almost to impossibility a successful imitation of him. I denied this, and contended that this very peculiarity made such imitation facile; and that, generally, the more marked and singular the style of a writer, the easier it was to produce a literary counterfeit of his productions.

A challenge to prove my position by such an imitation of Poe, followed the argument, and "The Raven" was selected as the poem to be paraphrased in style and rhythm.

Under this challenge I composed the "*Fire Fiend*," and, its public success being part of the bargain, I sent it to the Editor of *Harper's Magazine* for publication.

He, however, while admitting its resemblance to Poe

in manner and treatment, considered the *Magazine* an unsuitable medium for its publication, and politely declined it. But he added that he had shown it to a literary acquaintance,—the Editor of the *New York Saturday Press*,—who would accept it for his paper if I was willing to give it him. I was wholly unacquainted with this gentleman at that time, but wrote him immediately, offering him the poem, gratuitously, for the *Saturday Press*, and it was published in that paper, on the 19th of November, 1859, with the following editorial note, in brackets, prefacing it, viz.:

" [We postpone several articles this week to make place for the following communication, which we print with the single remark, that we 'don't see it.']"

From that date to the present moment, I have never seen the poem, in type, in the columns of any newspaper or other publication, save in the *New York Leader* of November 19th, 1864; nor have I ever offered it to any one, directly or indirectly. Nor, finally, had I heard of its ever having been offered to any such newspaper or publication, until the perusal of Dr. MACKENZIE'S articles in the *Philadelphia Press* gave me the startling information that for "several years" *I* had (wholly unknown to myself) been "sending the '*Fire Fiend*' to various newspapers and magazines," including his own journal. This statement of the Doctor's is perfectly consistent with the general accuracy and ingenuousness displayed throughout his remarks on the same subject.

The "*Fire Fiend*," then, was written as a hoax, published as a hoax, with an editorial remark sufficiently indicating the fact to any reader of fair perspicacity; and, as no money was asked, nor received for or by its publication, and no efforts whatever made to disseminate or perpetuate the hoax, either by its publisher or author, I feel no hesitation in pronouncing it, and in believing that my readers will pronounce it, to have been a venial and harmless literary joke, instead of an "unjustifiable fraud," "forgery," and a "great wrong," as it is solemnly declared to be by Dr. R. (RHADAMANTHUS?) SHELTON MACKENZIE!

C. D. G.

www.ingramcontent.com/pod-product-compliance
Lightning Source LLC
Chambersburg PA
CBHW020707260626
47157CB00008B/3175